Sprouted

Alex Westhaven

Sprouted
ISBN 978-1-937477-35-6
Copyright © 2013 Alex Westhaven
Published by Brazen Snake Books
All rights reserved.

Edited by Carol R. Ward

Also by the Author

Lettuce Prey

Jack

Angel Eyes

No Hazard Pay

Chapter One

Amelia used a sharp hand cultivator to scratch another set of lines into the soil underneath her prized roses. Reaching into the bag beside her, she scooped some bonemeal she'd harvested herself into a cup, and sprinkled it in the depressions she'd made. Pushing the soil back into place, she pushed up from her knees with some effort. The old joints weren't quite what they used to be, sadly.

She put her tools away and went inside, washing her hands in the kitchen sink. Tiny specks of dirt and grime ran down the drain, only to appear again as the water backed up and began to fill the stained porcelain basin.

"Oh fudge," she said, turning the water off. Third time in two weeks the dang thing had plugged up. It was her own fault though, washing pots and garden tools in the house. If she could just remember to use the hose...

She got the plunger from under the sink and thrust it against the drain with all her strength, but it wasn't long before her fingers started to ache and sweat rolled down her cheek. Shaking her head, she left the useless tool floating in the dirty water and picked up the phone to call Stan.

****

Twenty minutes later, the doorbell rang. She flung open the door with as much of a smile as she could muster. A large bald man that looked strikingly like the cartoon one on cleaning commercials stood outside, a beat up metal tool box in hand.

"Thanks for coming so soon. I think I might have finally killed the kitchen drain, but I promise if you can fix it, I'll be forever in your debt."

He laughed and shook his finger at her. "You know I don't work for free, Amelia. There won't be any debt, because I'm not leaving until you pay me. So unless you want me moving in..." He winked, crossing the threshold and making the room seem small with his bulk in the space.

She closed the door and followed the man through the living room and into the kitchen.

"I don't need a man around here full-time," she teased as she watched him inspect the sink. "And you probably don't need a woman watching you work, so I'll just be in the living room, if you need me."

He waved over his shoulder as he opened the cupboard under the sink and got down on his knees.

"Fine, fine. Just abandon me. If I drown, you pay my wife."

Amelia laughed. "She'll probably pay me, I bet," she parried as she walked away, moving into the living room to sit in her easy chair. Pointing the clicker at the TV across the room, she watched as the picture materialized and started clicking the channel button. It was more fun surfing through the pictures and colors than staring at that stupid guide grid.

A terracotta head sporting a thick mane of tiny plants caught her eye, and she stopped to watch the commercial. Dull orange pottery shapes of all sorts were soaked in water, and then parts of them smeared with what looked like a gelatinous substance that sprouted into a full head or body of a fluffy, living mat.

Amelia glanced down the hall. She could just barely see Stan's bald head as he sat on the floor, one of the pipes from her sink in hand. Imagining what he'd look like with a thick, lush chia bed on his shiny dome made her smile.

"Wouldn't it be fun if humans could grow plants on their heads?" she murmured, turning her attention back to the TV. It would be a wonderfully symbiotic relationship, like the bone meal she harvested for her roses, though that was more of a sacrificial relationship.

Stan came out of the kitchen, toolbox in hand. "There you go, Amelia. All fixed. Do I need to lecture you about washing off your gardening tools in the sink again?" He raised an eyebrow, looking stern though they both knew it was all an act.

She shook her head and coyly flipped her wrist down. "You know better than that, dear boy. But I'll try to do better this time. What do I owe you?" She got up and went to the table by the door and got her wallet out of her purse.

"For you, twenty-five. And I want you to know that's a special rate, so don't go telling your friends."

She laughed and pulled out the cash, handing him two bills. "It'll be our secret. You're too good to me, Stan. Now skedaddle so I can go make dinner. I still have some things to attend out in the shed tonight."

He took the money and waved as he walked out the door, and she waited until he pulled out of the driveway to lock the door behind him. Checking the clock, she went to the kitchen and took the brown pitcher out of the fridge, then let herself out the back door.

When she reached the shed, Amelia set the pitcher on a table next to the door while she got the key out of her pocket. Glancing around to make sure no one had come into the yard, she opened the padlock and hooked it through the metal clasp before grabbing the pitcher and going inside. Pulling the door shut behind her, she used a slide lock to ensure no one could enter, and then turned to what she liked to call her "garden brigade".

"Hello boys," she said with a smile. "It's time for dinner!"

There was no response, but that was a good thing. Moving toward the first stall, she poured the thick concoction her husband had perfected into the feeding container and watched it run down the feeding tube and into Number One. The man twitched a little against his bindings - they all did at first, but the flow was regulated to go slowly so it wouldn't gag the poor things.

She checked the bandage at the bottom of his left leg, where she'd harvested his foot two days ago. It hadn't bled through, which was a relief, but she'd need to change the wrapping and make sure it wasn't getting infected. The IV was still dripping steadily into his arm, delivering the herbal recipe she'd gotten from an eastern gentleman one year when they were traveling. It kept the brigade in a semi-comatose state, unaware of their surroundings for the most part and free of pain. She'd added extra garlic to Number One's mixture, to inhibit infection, and so far it seemed to be working.

Moving on, she fed the remaining three brigade members and then set the pitcher by the door. Picking up a small rake and shovel, she raked the small piles of excrement from each stall and put them into a bucket. Spreading fresh straw underneath the specially-made pallet beds, she tidied up each space and then helped each brigade member to lie down.

Early on in their studies, she and her husband had determined that changing positions during the day improved circulation and bodily functions, enabling the brigade members to live longer and be more productive. So every morning and evening they were repositioned, though she wouldn't be able to do it for much longer. Her strength seemed to be waning and it made her want to cry. Her husband had left his work to her, but who would take over when she was gone?

Shaking off the depressing thought, she went to a desk at the far end of the shed and sat down, opening the log book and marking down her notes for the day. She thought for a minute, bringing the end of the pen to her lips. Scanning the entries again, she finally made a new notation for Numbers Two and Three before closing the book. Her last experiment would begin tomorrow. And after it was over, she'd write up her findings and lay the brigade to rest, once and for all.

Chapter Two

The next morning Amelia got up with the sun and took a long hot shower. She found some chia seeds in the cupboard and mixed them with a few tablespoons of water, letting them sit as she prepared the brigade's food for the day. As the seeds absorbed water they swelled, each growing into a thick, clear bubble around a tiny black heart. Together they formed a light paste, and Amelia took the pitcher and bowl out to the shed.

Once the morning chores were done and the brigade was upright once more, she prepped her subjects' heads by shaving them close and putting a thick band of toweling at the crown to catch any overflow. Then with a sharp knife she made tiny shallow cuts lengthwise across each scalp, about an inch apart. Taking her soaked chia seeds, she smeared the concoction over their heads just like on the commercials. When they each had a good layer mingled with the blood oozing from the shallow wounds, she fitted a clear plastic shower cap over each head and then turned on the grow lights above, directing them slightly to the side to avoid overheating. Going to the desk, she got the instant camera she kept around just for such occasions and snapped a photo of them both, adding the pictures to the log book with a short entry for each. Her duties done, she turned her attention to Number Four, who seemed to be having a difficult time breathing.

"I'm afraid your time is about up, m'dear." She'd left him prone in preparation for his death, and now she examined every inch of his skin, looking for any sign of disease or rot. Not that it mattered too much - he would be laid to rest in the bottom of their huge compost pile to return to the earth like those who had come before, but if there was no obvious sign of disease, she'd chip up his limbs for the flower bed first.

She sat back and stared at him for a moment, such a peaceful expression on his gaunt face. How long he would last was anyone's guess - she'd seen them hang on for days in such a condition, but most only had a few hours. Checking her watch, she noted that it was still early. It took time and energy to butcher a body, but as long as she had a good breakfast and didn't forget to stop for lunch, she should have time today.

Patting his shoulder, she went to the desk and made an entry into the logbook as to his disposal. With one last look at Numbers Two and Three to make sure the towel-bands were catching the blood, she went back to the house for breakfast.

As she opened the back door she heard the doorbell ringing and frowned. Who on earth would be calling at such an early hour? She made her way through the house and peeked out the side window, surprised to find a rather large man holding hands with a pretty little girl on her doorstep.

She opened the door and smiled, trying to ignore her growling stomach.

"Good morning," she said, smiling pointedly at the little girl before she looked up at the man. "What can I do for the two of you?"

He returned her smile, his soft expression at odds with his muscular bulk.

"We were out walking, and Andrea here saw your roses. She has a question for you." He turned to the little girl and nodded. "Go ahead."

"I was just wondering if I could have one of your pretty flowers for my room. The pink ones remind me of my mom." The little girl raised her eyebrows, big green eyes staring hopefully.

Amelia's heart melted. "Of course you can, my dear. Let me just get my pruning shears and a damp paper towel to wrap the stems in while you carry them home." She went to the kitchen and was back in two minutes, joining the girl and her father on the front sidewalk.

"The pink ones, you say?" Amelia asked. An enthusiastic nod from the little girl, and Amelia was on her knees. She cut one large, open bloom and several smaller blooms just beginning to open. Wrapping the ends, she secured the damp paper towel around them with a rubber band and presented the small bouquet to Andrea.

"There. I bet your mother will love those. Is she waiting for you at home?"

The girl's eyes turned sad. "She doesn't live with us anymore - she died. We're going to visit her at the cemetery."

Amelia blinked back tears. "I'm sorry to hear that your mother's gone already. I hope the flowers bring you both joy. Did your mother grow roses?"

Andrea shook her head, dropping her gaze to the ground.

"We have one of her bushes left," the dad said, putting a hand on each of the girl's shoulders. "Unfortunately, I'm not very good with plants, so I'm afraid it's just barely limping along. I'm sure it needs something, but I'm not sure what, exactly."

Amelia started to stand, and the man helped her up. "If you can wait here for just another minute, I'll be right back with something that will make your roses grow like gangbusters." She followed the front path where it branched off toward the side of the house. Opening the cellar doors, she grabbed the flashlight that always sat just on the top step and went down into the cool dirt room. She retrieved a small jar and took it back up to the yard, handing it to the man.

"Now this is pretty potent stuff - I make it myself. Just sprinkle a third of a cup around the base of the plant once a week or even every two weeks, and water it in well. That's all you need to do and your roses will be looking great in no time."

Andrea smiled and clapped, as well as she could with the cut flowers in her hand, and the man smiled.

"How much do we owe you?"

Amelia shook her head with a slight laugh. "Oh nothing at all. It's on the house."

She waved at the man and his daughter as they walked away down the sidewalk. How lovely they'd been to chat with. Perhaps they'd stop by again some day and let her know how the rose bush was doing.

With a wistful sigh, she went back inside and started to make breakfast, hoping she would still have enough time to dispose of Number Four and replace the jar of fertilizer she'd just given away.

Chapter Three

It was four in the afternoon when she finally finished with Number Four. The backhoe needed work, but she'd managed to limp it along enough to dig out a hole in the compost mound and bury the parts that weren't needed immediately. While she was at it, she'd turned the rest of the pile, satisfied with the heat coming off the collection of old leaves, grass, garden waste and other organic refuse. There had even been enough new soil under one end to fill a barrel and bring back to the house. She'd use it to refresh the soil in the vegetable gardens tomorrow.

She took a quick shower, scrubbing away the day's labor and wondering how her chia experiment was doing. If the little plants sprouted it would be ground-breaking, really. Another article to write up for the research files. Someday, she'd publish them and the gardening world would be turned on it's head at their discoveries. It was the ultimate recycling program, really, as well as an alternate way to get use out of transients and prisoners. No reason they couldn't be productive members of society after all, using the methods she and her husband had developed.

Toweling off, she dressed in clean clothes and went to the kitchen. After a quick sandwich for dinner, she prepared food for the brigade and went to the shed, anxious to check for any growth though she knew it was really too soon.

She fed the brigade and checked Numbers Two and Three for any signs of growth, but found nothing but little black seeds. She arranged them as comfortably as she could, but they would have to remain upright for the duration, which worried her. Chia was supposed to sprout within a couple of days though, so hopefully they'd be resting comfortably again before long.

She cleaned out the stalls and spread new straw, wistful when she got to the fourth enclosure. While she wasn't anywhere near death yet herself, she just couldn't see taking in another brigade member without knowing he would be cared for after she was gone. It was her one regret in life, not having found someone who might want to keep the project going.

Resigned, she cleaned and scrubbed out the stall until it was pristine, and then removed all the other apparatus used to keep the brigade members alive and functioning. Everything was thoroughly cleaned and sterilized before being stowed in a trunk near the door of the stall.

It was nearly ten by the time she finished, and when she finally locked herself back in the house she was exhausted. A quick glass of milk and a couple of cookies she'd made the weekend before, and she was ready for bed.

****

The next morning she rose and prepared the brigade's breakfast, not quite ready to eat yet herself. She walked out to the shed, her mind not yet fully awake as she approached the outbuilding, and realized the door was ajar.

Amelia nearly dropped the serving tray when she peered through the small opening and realized someone was standing just inside...

The interloper was short, Amelia realized. Too short to be an adult, and wearing a dress as well. She wasn't sure what to do - they'd never taken a child before, but she couldn't risk anyone finding out about their research before it was ready to be shared.

The girl wasn't screaming. Upon closer inspection, child looked to be examining Number Two with a rather analytical expression that reminded Amelia of her late husband. An idea began to form, one that was risky, but potentially just what they all needed.

Amelia swung the door open slowly, smiling when the young girl turned toward her. It was the girl who had been at her door the other day.

"Good morning...Andrea, isn't it?" she said, stepping up into the shed. "It's nice to see you again, dear, but what are you doing back here?"

The girl looked down at her toes, nervously clasping her hands together. "I knocked on the front door, but no one answered, so I came around to see if you were working in your garden."

Amelia smiled, going down on one knee to put her at the girl's level. "This shed is normally locked, my dear - how did you get in?"

"The lock wasn't closed all the way. I'm sorry. I didn't mean to be nosy. My dad always says I'm too nosy..."

Amelia laughed, reaching out to pat the girl's arm. "It's okay, honey. But you know you can't tell anyone about my experiments here, right? Most people wouldn't understand."

"I won't tell. What are your 'speriments, anyway? They look like people, sort of." Andrea turned to look at Number Two again, tilting her head as if another angle might help.

Amelia stood up, considering how much she should say. Clearly the girl didn't realize exactly what she was looking at, and maybe that was for the best. For now, at least.

"Well, they're a different sort of people," Amelia said. "I call them my Garden Brigade, and they help me grow things. Do you remember the fertilizer I gave you?"

Andrea nodded.

"They helped me make that. They're kind of like my secret garden helpers." She pointed to the tray she'd brought in. "Would you like to see how I feed them?"

"Sure." Andrea nodded her head again. "How did you find them?"

Amelia retrieved the pitcher of pureed food and went to Number One's stall. She set up the feeding tube and poured in the measured amount of breakfast.

"I don't really find them," she said as Andrea watched the liquid flow through the clear tube and into Number One's mouth. "They seem to find me, when the time is right." She moved to the next stall, and Andrea followed. Amelia fed Number Two and then set the pitcher down to examine his head. To her delight, tiny little green leaves were emerging from the chia seeds underneath the plastic.

"Would you like to see something neat?" she asked. Andrea. The girl nodded, and Amelia motioned for her to come closer. Carefully removing the plastic, Amelia lifted her up so she could see the seedlings.

"Wow!" Andrea said, her mouth pursing into a dramatic "O". It had been a long time since Amelia had been around children. Too long, perhaps.

"Those are baby plants," she said, putting the girl down. "Number Two is helping me start them, and if our experiment works, he'll provide nutrients for them until they're big enough to plant in the ground."

Andrea's eyes were wide. "Wow," she said again. "He can do that?"

Amelia nodded. "I think so, but like I said, it's just an experiment. And we can't tell anyone just yet, in case it doesn't work. Not even your daddy, okay?"

The girl nodded solemnly. "I won't tell anyone. I promise. Can I come back and see when the plants are bigger?"

"We'll see." Amelia picked up the pitcher and went to Number Three's stall. "Why don't you help me finish my chores here, and then we'll have lunch, if you don't think your dad will mind."

"He's at work," Andrea said. "And I don't have school today."

"Well then, that's perfect. We'll call and let him know where you are when we go in the house so he doesn't worry. Now why don't you grab that bucket and rake over there. You can help me tidy up the stalls a bit."

Chapter Four

Andrea came by every morning that week to check on the brigade and help Amelia with the chores before school. Amelia was hesitant at first - she'd thought to make the girl an apprentice, but there was the father to consider. Eventually, he'd be curious, and that would be awkward, to say the least. She couldn't expect the girl to lie indefinitely to family either - that would be wrong.

So Amelia accepted the help, but only to a point. On the day that she harvested Number One's other foot to chip up for more fertilizer, she'd told Andrea to take a day off. The girl was disappointed, but it was better to keep some things a secret. For now, at least.

It wasn't long before the chia sprouts were big enough to plant in the garden. Andrea had finished the morning clean-up and was waiting with a plastic container lined with damp paper towels and a tiny pair of stamp tongs, which Amelia thought might work best for removing the baby plants from Number Two's scalp.

"Ready?" Amelia asked, placing a chair next to Number Two for her helper to stand on. The girl nodded, and Amelia helped her up, reaching for the tongs.

"I'll do the first couple, and then you can do a few, okay? We need to be slow and gentle. Do you think you can do that?"

Andrea nodded. "I'll do my best."

Amelia poured a small amount of water over Number Two's head for a little extra lubrication. Then she grasped the base of a Chia sprout with the tongs and gently tugged. The sprout came free with only slight resistance. She smiled, laying it in the container.

"There. That wasn't so bad. Let me do a few more, just to make sure there won't be any snags."

Working methodically, she pulled out five more random baby plants from different points on Number Two's head.

"See how the roots look strong and healthy?" She held one of the sprouts up for Angela to examine, careful not to squeeze the tongs too hard. "And the leaves are perfectly round and bright green. That's exactly what we want to see." She laid the plant with the others, and then handed the tongs to Andrea.

"Now it's your turn. Be gentle - don't squeeze the tongs too hard."

Andrea nodded, her face serious as she very slowly grasped a plant at the base and pulled it off of the scalp. Holding it up she smiled, though in her excitement she squeezed too hard. They both watched as the sprout broke in two, falling to the floor.

"I'm sorry," she said, her eyes moistening. "I didn't mean to ruin it..."

Amelia laughed, wrapping an arm around the girl's shoulders for a quick squeeze. "It's okay, m'dear. It takes practice, and we have plenty of plants. Why don't you keep working on Number Two, and I'll go see about Number Three. You might be less nervous if I'm not watching."

Andrea shook her head. "But I don't want to ruin any more! Please, you do it. I can't."

Amelia took the tongs, frowning. "You know it's okay to break things once in awhile, don't you? It's often the best way to learn how to do something - by doing it wrong. Why do you think we do experiments?"

Andrea shrugged. "My dad says we should get things right the first time. Otherwise there's no point in doing them."

"Well your dad is wrong about that - if you're afraid to fail, you'll never actually do anything. And that would be a shame." She took the girl's hand and placed the tongs back in them.

"I want you to finish pulling the rest of these, and I don't care how many you break. Just do your best, and I bet you'll save more than you drop. The key thing to remember is to not leave any behind, and I'm pretty sure you can handle that, right?"

Andrea looked at the little plants, clearly dubious. "I guess so."

Amelia smiled again and patted her shoulder. "You'll do just fine, and I'll be right on the other side of the wall with Number Three if you need anything. Now let's get to work so we can go plant these in the garden."

She took a few steps and then turned back, watching Andrea tentatively reach out with the tongs and grab another plant. She held it up and then put it in the container before moving to pull another one.

Amelia went to the desk and got another container and a pair of tongs, entering the stall with Number Three. Starting to pull the sprouts from Number Three's scalp, she grinned as Andrea began to sing quietly on the other side of the wall.

****

It was several hours before all the Chia sprouts were planted in a special section of Amelia's garden. She'd cleared a rectangle of space and put a wooden frame of two by fours with screen on top over it to protect the small plants from critters that might decide to snack. Waving goodbye to Andrea, she went back into the shed. She hadn't said anything to her helper, but there were signs of impending infection on both Number Two and Number Three's heads, and she needed to clean them up and change their positions as soon as possible. It seemed that what was good for the chia sprouts might not be so good for the Garden Brigade...

She carefully cleaned each head with a strong vinegar mixture, and then covered the open wounds with a homemade salve of beeswax, sweet almond oil and chamomile. Gently wrapping the heads in soft strips of cotton, she laid her charges down on fresh beds of straw and went to the house to get their dinner. Grinding up extra fresh garlic for a boost of natural antibiotics, she fed the brigade and then locked the shed for the night. Exhausted, she heated up a TV dinner and collapsed into her recliner to eat and rest.

The news came on a little later, and she turned up the volume as police lights flashed outside a neat little suburban home with lovely manicured gardens. Or they'd been lovely at some point. It looked like they'd been neglected for quite some time, and Amelia leaned forward as the camera zoomed in on a small figure wearing a familiar lavender twinset and jeans, standing by one of the police cruisers.

"It was so quick," Andrea said in a shaky voice. "One minute were having a nice dinner, and the next those men were coming through the back door. Dad told me to duck under the table, so I did. After they left, I saw the blood..."

The girl stopped, turning away and the camera panned out to the news reporter. Apparently three men had broken in, hit her father over the head hard enough to knock him unconscious, and stolen every piece of electrical equipment within reach.

The reporter blinked hard, apparently fighting tears. Amelia's heart broke for the child. As the reporter droned on about a rash of burglaries in the neighborhood and how people should take care to keep their property secure, Amelia got up and turned the TV off. Pulling on a jacket, she got her keys and went outside, stopping at the sidewalk to look around for any sign of flashing lights. Andrea normally walked to her house, so they had to live close.

A red and blue hue to the east caught her attention, and she walked one block up and another block over before seeing the police cruisers in the street. Making her way down the sidewalk, she was stopped by one of the officers. She began to explain, but there was no need as Andrea lifted her head and their eyes met.

The girl ran to her, ducking under the police tape and throwing her arms around Amelia's waist.

"Did you see what they did to my dad? I don't know what to do!"

Amelia held her, stroking her back, and she could feel her protective instincts kicking in.

"It'll be okay, m'dear. Let's make sure your dad is okay." She looked up at the officer. "Can I take her to the hospital?"

"Who are you?" he asked. She started to answer, but Andrea beat her to it.

"She's my grandma," the girl said, not even missing a beat. "She'll take care of me." She turned to Amelia and winked. Who could resist that hopeful look in her eye.

The officer used his radio for a moment, and then nodded. "I'll need your contact information, ma'am - in case we need to get a hold of either of you. Then you can go."

Amelia gave him her phone number and address, forcing herself not to hesitate though it made her nervous. If the police came to the house...but she couldn't think about that right now. Andrea was all that mattered.

Finally they were released, and after they walked back to Amelia's house she drove Andrea to the hospital.

It wasn't long before the doctor met them in the waiting room.

Chapter Five

"Please don't send me away," Andrea begged several days later. Child services was at the door with a second cousin of Andrea's father. The woman wanted to raise Andrea with her other two daughters, and as much as Amelia wanted to keep Andrea with her, she knew that this young, soft-spoken mother would be able to give her things that Amelia simply couldn't.

Amelia smiled, and hugged the girl close. "Oh honey. You don't want to live with an old woman like me. Georgia and her husband can give you a good life and a lot of things I really can't." She looked up at Georgia, who stood off to the side.

"You'll let her come visit me, won't you?"

The other woman nodded. "Of course she can, anytime she wants. The bus runs right past our house, and I saw a stop at the end of the block. It won't be any trouble at all."

Amelia nodded, and looked back at her young charge. "You go with Georgia now, and get settled into your new home. Come and see me this weekend, and I'll have a surprise for you, okay?"

Obviously reluctant, the girl nodded. "If you say so, I guess I'll try." She went upstairs to get her bag and Georgia came over to take Amelia's hand.

"You've been so wonderful taking care of her like this. I can't tell you how much we appreciate it, and you're always welcome to visit us too. I'll make sure Andrea has a bus pass by this weekend. Thank you so much for everything."

Amelia smiled and patted the woman's hand. "It's no trouble at all - Andrea's a special girl. We'll all get through this, it will just take some time."

Andrea came down the stairs, backpack over her shoulder and ran to Amelia, enveloping her in a big hug.

"I love you Amelia," she whispered. "I'll be back soon."

Amelia blinked back tears. She never would have guessed how dear this girl would become in such a short time.

"I love you too." She reached into her pocket and pulled out two keys she'd taken from her husband's old keyring that morning. "I want you to have these. That way you can come and go as you please." She looked into Andrea's eyes, and felt the connection they had. She understood the full meaning of the gift, and nodded solemnly.

"I'll keep them safe," she said, turning to follow Georgia out the door.

Amelia watched them go, waving from the front step until the dark sedan was out of sight. Moving back inside, she locked the door and went to her desk, pulling a folder out of the top drawer.

Examining the three sketches Andrea had helped her draw, she retrieved a couple of yellowed cards from her husband's old Rolodex and picked up the phone. The men who'd murdered Andrea's father wouldn't be a burden on society much longer. It was time for them to give back.

****

Amelia groaned when the alarm went off early Saturday morning. The sun was barely up, and her entire body hurt, but she knew she had to get moving if she wanted everything to be perfect by the time Andrea arrived.

One of her husband's old contacts had come through once she'd explained what she wanted, and things had moved more quickly than she'd expected. It had been a long and exhausting few days, and she knew she'd pushed herself too hard. But it would be worth it when Andrea saw what she'd done.

Throwing back the covers, she took a shower that turned out to be longer than she'd planned, but the warm water felt good on her aching muscles. Dressing quickly, she went downstairs and ate a quick breakfast before preparing a pitcher for the brigade. Setting up the coffee pot to be ready when she came in, she went out to the shed and completed the morning chores with more enthusiasm than she actually felt. Then she made sure everything was ready for Andrea's surprise before going back to the house for coffee and a newspaper break.

Three hours passed, then four, then five. Amelia did her nightly chores, growing more depressed by the minute. She'd expected the girl to forget her eventually, getting caught up in school and friends and all the other things young people do while they're young enough to enjoy them. But so soon? She hadn't expected this. Part of her hoped that Andrea had at least hidden the shed keys well. In hindsight, Amelia knew she should have waited to give them. Youngsters could be so fickle.

Darkness fell, and Amelia finally decided to call Georgia, just to make sure Andrea was safe. That's what she told herself, though surely someone would have called if there had been an accident.

The phone rang for a long time, but no one picked up. Not even an answering machine. Amelia frowned as she disconnected the call, a bad feeling growing in her stomach.

She got online and typed Georgia's full name into a search page. There were no results, but that wasn't alarming by itself. Plenty of people weren't online, though Amelia wasn't sure why.

She typed in Andrea's name, and went to her blog. The last entry was the day before she went home with Georgia. Nothing after.

The phone rang and she was relieved to see Georgia's number on the caller ID.

"Andrea? Is that you? I've been so worried," she said. There was a slight pause and her relief faded as she sensed it wasn't Andrea on the other end of the line.

"Amelia," Georgia said, her voice husky. "I didn't have your number, or I would have called much sooner. There's been a terrible accident, and Andrea is in the hospital."

Amelia sat down, her legs shaking as she closed her eyes and asked the obvious questions.

"Is she okay? What happened, and when?"

Another long pause told Amelia all she needed to know.

"The doctors say she'll live, but she's never going to be herself again. She was walking to the school bus stop and there was a driver not paying attention...she went so far, and hit her head so hard...I can't believe she didn't die, honestly. I'm so sorry. I feel just horrible..."

The woman broke down, sobbing in Amelia's ear and Amelia disconnected the call, letting the phone slip onto her lap. All of her hopes for the future were gone along with the only friend she had left. Tears ran down her face as she thought of her little rose-loving friend lying in a cold, sterile hospital room, no doubt hooked up to a million different wires and tubes. Was that how she'd spend the rest of her life? And how long would that be now? Was it life, really?

She wiped her eyes on a nearby blanket and took a few deep, calming breaths. It was horribly tragic, and if she'd just kept the girl there with her, maybe it wouldn't have happened. But there was only one thing she could do now. A gift she could give to the girl who had brought so much joy to her life in such a short time. She just needed to confirm the diagnosis and see Andrea with her own eyes.

Visiting hours were over, no doubt, and Amelia went to bed with a heavy heart, tossing and turning until the sun peeked through the bedroom curtains again. She went to the window and leaned against the frame, watching the sunrise and pondering the ways she could accomplish all that needed to be done.

****

It was after noon before Amelia finally made it to the hospital. As she walked through the doors, a tiny ray of hope still remained in her heart that perhaps

Georgia had been wrong. Perhaps the doctors had erred on the side of caution and Amelia would be sitting up, laughing, waiting to see her.

Or maybe it was bad, but Amelia would still be able to function. She'd just need help in life, and Amelia was prepared to offer her services as permanent caretaker, should that be the case.

Alas, when she reached the correct room, her worse fears were confirmed. Georgia and two teen girls stood on the other side of the bed, decidedly weepy. A tall, average-looking man sat in an armchair on the other hand, looking rather bored. In the center of it all was Andrea, so little in the center of the bed, with a breathing tube in her mouth and various other tubes and cables attached to her body here and there.

"Amelia - you made it!" Georgia rushed across the room to envelope her in a hug, though it felt fake. Amelia patted the woman on the back, resisting the urge to push her away.

"We weren't sure you'd get here in time," Georgia said, straightening up and swiping at her eyes. "We've decided to take her off life support. The doctor said she won't ever recover, and...oh, it's just so horrible! After all she's been through, too..."

Amelia nodded carefully. "May I speak with the doctor briefly first?"

Georgia exchanged a quick look with the man who was presumably her husband, and then gave a curt nod and a dramatic sniff.

"Of course, but please don't be long. We don't want her suffering to last any longer than it has to. Dr. Howard is the one you're looking for."

Amelia nodded in return, suppressing a triumphant grin. Dr. Howard was an old friend, and something was definitely not right here. He would help her, regardless of what needed to happen next.

She went to the nurses station and asked to speak with the doctor, then waited in the hall for him to arrive. It wasn't long before he appeared, glancing toward Andrea's room and motioning for Amelia to follow him.

When they reached his office, he closed the door after her.

"It's so good to see you, Amelia. It's been years. How are you, and how did you come to be involved with Andrea?"

"It's good to see you too, David." She took the offered seat and nodded as he situated himself behind the desk. "It has been years - too long, really. And I'm doing well for the most part, except that little girl in there. She's my friend, and I'm worried that things may not quite be what they seem at the moment."

His drawn brows and serious gaze told her she was on the right track, unfortunately.

"Well, I doubt she was hit by a car. The injuries to her torso and thighs where an impact like that would have occurred are actually minimal. Her head, however..." He looked down for a moment, and then sighed. "The family asked me not to share this with anyone, but I was planning to call the police after they left today. Your involvement...changes things, of course."

Amelia nodded. "Go on."

"When you fall, you can't actually hit the part of her head where we found the depression in her skull. The back or sides of the head would hit first. But just there, at the top of the spinal column? You'd have to land on something, or fall back into something vertical...or..."

"...or someone would have to hit you with something." Amelia leaned back in her chair, blowing out a long breath. "Someone hit her."

Dr. Howard nodded. "Hard enough to damage both her spinal column and her brain, it looks like. The base of the skull fractured into pieces, several of them driven deep into her brain by the force. If she does wake up, which I highly doubt, she'll be both paralyzed and vegetative."

Amelia blinked back the moisture in her eyes. "She only went to live with that family a few days ago - and I haven't heard from her since. If I had just let her live with me..."

"There was no way to know - and you thought you were doing what's best," the doctor said. He paused for a moment, his expression thoughtful. "I don't think there's any way to look into this without attracting undo attention to you, unfortunately, since you were close to Andrea. And I assume you're still studying alternate gardening theories?"

"Yes. But not for much longer. I just can't keep up with the work. Andrea was helping me, actually, and I'd hoped...but now she's gone." The tears escaped then, and she wiped her face, trying to maintain some semblance of control.

Dr. Howard came around the desk and sat in the chair next to her, squeezing her shoulders.

"What if I made a little arrangement with the morgue - one last time, so you can lay her to rest in a more respectful, fitting way than those idiots out there ever could? Would that help? And then perhaps if you still have your old contacts..."

His soothing voice helped to calm her tears, and she nodded, accepting the tissue he offered. It was fate, of course, that out of all the doctors in the hospital he had been the one to care for Andrea in her final hours. A sign that the plans she'd already prepared for had come together so easily.

"Yes. That would be truly wonderful," Amelia said quietly. "I loved that girl like my own, even though I didn't know her long, and I'd like to keep her close." She gently blew her nose, and the doctor patted her back with an understanding smile.

"It's settled then," he said in a normal, professional tone. "Will you be staying for the finale, or shall I give the family your condolences?"

Amelia considered the question for a long moment.

"Please give them my condolences," she said finally, rising from the chair. "I think my time might be better spent elsewhere, all things considered."

"Very well." Dr. Howard held out a hand, and she shook it, finding comfort in his warm grip. "Your delivery should be there around eight this evening, if that's okay."

She nodded, her lips turning up slightly. "Just about sunset. That will be perfect."

Making her way home, the information on Andrea's injuries bothered Amelia. The men who had killed the child's father were no longer a threat, and hadn't been for days. Given that the doctor would have shared his findings with the family, why hadn't they told her the truth? And why hadn't they called the police to investigate?

There was only one reason they'd want to cover up the real reason behind Andrea's death. And no possible way for Amelia to discover the one person actually responsible for the blow.

With a heavy heart, she laid her things in the entry way and went to her desk, sitting for what felt like hours before she finally reached for the card file. One last time, she flipped through the cards, feeding most of them through a small electric shredder on the desk until she found the one she sought. She hesitated again before dialing the phone, and fifteen minutes later, she shredded that card too, along with all of the others.

****

When the doorbell rang at precisely eight that evening, Amelia was ready. She showed the two men where to put the body and then tipped them both generously. After they left, she opened the bag and caressed Andrea's pale, cold face.

"It's okay, darling. They will pay for what they did, and you...you will be with me always, making the garden more beautiful than ever." She smiled, wiping a stray tear and then running her fingers along the stitched cuts where the body had been prepared. Then she picked up the body and carried it out to the garden, laying her gently, reverently, into a deep trench just barely large enough that she'd dug behind the rose bushes.

Covering the girl with a length of thin cotton, she stood back as the sun turned the clouds fiery with oranges and pinks, murmuring a prayer that the girl would rest easy and nourish the earth to bring beauty in her stead. As the last rays of light were fading, Amelia filled in the trench and scattered a generous handful of chia seeds over the damp earth, finishing with a frame of wood and wire to keep the plot well protected.

Loathe to leave, she forced herself to go check on the brigade, and then went into the house. Moving automatically, she went through her nightly routine, barely noticing anything at all as she prepared for bed. She'd just turned out the lights when the phone rang.

Picking up the receiver, she held it to her ear.

"It's done. Car wreck. No survivors."

She closed her eyes, her muscles relaxing and a sense of peace embracing her soul.

"Thank you."

###

About the Author

Alex Westhaven resides in Billings, Montana with her husband and two over-sized lap dogs. Halloween is her favorite holiday, and she has more than her fair share of skeletons (and other body parts) in the closet. Stop by AlexWesthaven.com for all the latest horror news and upcoming books.